maico morellini

INN OF THE SURVIVORS

translated by
rose facchini

INN OF THE SURVIVORS

1

THE last few kilometers, the ones that change the atmosphere of the forest and transform it into a swamp, are the most difficult to cross. The deep verdure of the trees and the dense shadows of the undergrowth turn branches and rocks into slippery traps.

You trip, one, two, three times.

"Christ." Your sputtered curse mixes with the rain, the drops engorged by their journey through the leaves and branches, falling to the ground like bombs. You are only seventeen, but you have learned to hide it. You have learned to act older. If someone were to look you in the eye, they might discover your true age, but nobody does. You do not want them to.

You slip again. You grasp a fern with your gloved hand and it keeps you from tumbling into the carpet of leaves. You keep your balance, half-kneeling, your ripped jeans brushing the ground.

You were told two days ago in Forlì, and you heard echoes of it yesterday in what must have once been Cesena: heading toward the Adriatic, the forest would lose its grip and become a mire of sand and mud.

But you were determined to get to the sea. After months and years of aimless wandering, you have decided to get to the sea. You heard about a place there, a place for people like you, and you want to find it no matter the cost.

"Besides, what do I have to lose?" you ask the cracked log. A beech tree. You know plants as well as you do animals. Recalling that name pains you because it belongs to a past that will never return, and that kind of past, when it is lost forever, can *really* hurt.

"It's better for everyone," you add. "For everyone." You get back on your feet with a pop of joints and you look up at the heavens.

Between the crowded branches over your head, braided like the woolen yarn with which your mother worked at the farm, you catch a glimpse of the overcast skies. A roiling swirl, black with thin, white striations, icy storm clouds that collide with one another. And then distant thunder and lightning that play no part in this storm.

It has been like this for weeks and that is why you decided to move into the forest. The rain is light, but without shelter it settles into your bones. Staying under the trees, on the other hand, is no longer dangerous. At least for the time being. Those flashes that are now making you squint have haunted the sky for a year, but the lightning had long since ceased. The log in front of you, a split mouth glistening like shattered glass, would perhaps beg to differ. But plants do not think. Lucky them.

It feels bumpy beneath your gloves. Resin and springy clumps of moss. Old wounds.

Wood and bark have somehow healed them, and you would like to be able to do the same with yourself. You pass your gloved hand over the root of your braid, then climb up to the base of your head: your wounds are hidden, but they are there. Under your hair. In your mind.

"Just some lightning," you mutter, looking up at the sky. "Just a…" A drop the size of your fist splats on your face, a cold slap that tears the words out of your mouth. As a little girl you thought this was freedom: facing the storms on the hilltops, challenging the atmosphere just when it went mad with a flawed being, to clash with snow, hail, and rain.

Now you enjoy small moments of nothingness and cold water on your face. Instants when you manage to concentrate only on what you feel on your skin and not on the grief inside. You feel the rivulets of water that trickle along the wrinkles that the weather has incised on your young skin, down your nose, your cheeks, and the rest.

You lick your lips. At least the rain here

tastes good. Not like in Bologna. There are so many *flawed* people near the big cities and the weather knows it.

The weather always knows.

This is why you are determined to head for the sea.

"C'mon." You set off again. The mud releases your boots with a greedy squelch followed by suction, water taking its place. You take a couple of steps, then look back. Your footprints have vanished. Sludge, bushes, rain, leaves; it seems that the world is doing everything in its power to forget about you, to erase any trace of your passage.

"And it should." You hear yourself in the silence of the undergrowth. You hear yourself for the first time in quite a while. Your voice has become hoarse, low, more similar to a growl than you remember. Not a girlish voice, but then again nothing in your life is how it should be. Life is not wandering in the Po Valley forest with a backpack and a few pouches of seeds, wearing dirty, ill-fitting clothes with wet hair plastered to your forehead. It is not talking to yourself. It is not escaping because you are not brave enough to end it all.

"No one's life is going the way it should," you remark while you search for a less marshy path out of the forest. The trees are changing all around you; beech trees give way to poplars, alders, English oaks. You know them all, those trees. They surrounded your home and from the top of the hill, from the farm, you could see all the Po Valley, all the green colors of the forest that had sprung up so quickly. Mom always insisted that you and your siblings learn the names of the trees by heart. It was one of those little things she truly cared about, one of those little rules that she enforced no matter what.

You start to feel a stinging sensation in your nose, and you thank the rain. You thank it because it dilutes the tears, because it quenches the salt. Because when you taste the pain, all that is wrong inside you resurfaces, working its way into your gut, in your thoughts, your memories. And you want nothing to do with your memories.

You find a dry ridge. No, not dry. Less sodden. You single it out for its tufts of dark green bushes that grow there, a sort of path where you will be able to move a little faster.

No one's life is going the way it should.

You realized this immediately after escaping the farm, and you have seen evidence of it time and again for three consecutive years. You deplore close proximity to cities. You disliked what you saw, but you needed information and there was no other place where you could search for it. The reality? Everyone tries to do what they can but no one's life, nobody's, is how it should be.

You jump from one bush to the next, the terrain more solid under your feet, and for a little while you manage to forget almost everything. You bend your knees, find your footing, push, muscles stretch and release the accumulated energy, a leap, then another. You are short of breath. The exertion helps distract you and for this reason you accept everything like a benediction.

You even smile. And you know the smile changes your face. If someone were to see you now—soaked braid that bounces on your back, brown backpack a little too small, puffer jacket, gloves, boots with purple laces—if someone were to see you now, they would think of a girl in the middle of some game. Nothing could be further from the truth.

When you stop, when you set your hands on your bent knees to catch your breath, the Po Valley forest is behind you and something in the air is changing.

There is a different smell, more humid and less oppressive than the rain that is now so fine as to resemble fog.

It is the sea. You have never been there, the ocean. Before escaping, you had never strayed too far from the farm except for school, but you know that this is how it smells. And you know the sea is an ancestral magnet, something that lures people on the run, something that calls you to it when no other place wants you, when it is you who does not want any other place.

You squint, little drops of condensation gather on your eyelashes, the silence of the plain so different from the live murmur of the forest that has accompanied you for three years. You look around without turning and you see a new marshy world that surrounds you.

Before you, far but you do not know how far, is a cluster of flickering lights. You already know this last stretch of road will be the most difficult to travel.

You were not mistaken. You take nearly the rest of the day to trudge through the area of swamp separating you from the destination of that aimless pilgrimage begun three years ago. You have needed to change course, retrace your steps, move forward, then reverse, and finally continue onward again. You have sunk in the muddy sand, lost a boot in the marsh, and when you arrive at the abandoned parking lot—a slab of cement speckled with large shrubs the size of cars—you are soaked from head to toe.

It is nearly sunset. You realize this from how the clouds on the horizon have begun to turn a pale yellow. That is the Sun's new pigment. A distant watercolor that seems to mock you, appearing only at sunrise and sunset, but always in the distance, always aloof. In Bologna, the generator salesman from whom you bought information told you that some days prior on the Futa Pass, after the birth of a *pure* child, the Sun had come out. Maybe a legend, maybe one of those prefabricated hopes one tells in urban shadows to pluck up courage, but you know that it is not *only* a legend. You really saw the Sun three years ago. You saw it and you discarded it like your old life.

Here it is. Beyond the parking lot, beyond the dilapidated seaside factory, beyond the beach with heaps of sand, algae, and shrubs:

here is the Inn of the Survivors. You see it before understanding what it is. Now that the day is about to die, the lights that have guided you thus far shine brighter: they are lamps fixed onto long poles. No, not poles, but trees of ships. You count five of them, different sizes, different lights. All turned toward the hinterland as if they were reverse beacons: they do not warn ships that there is land in sight but inform the Po Valley fugitives that they have arrived at sea.

You cross the parking lot and walking on the asphalt makes you feel strange. It is hard, solid. After all those months spent mostly on the soft and unstable ground of the forest, finding such sturdy support almost makes you lose your balance. Like when you dismount from a horse after having been in the saddle the entire afternoon.

The farm again. The past again. You worry at your lower lip, nervous, and you only now realize that it has almost stopped raining. The sea seems to oppose the fallout that accompanied the climate, in the end mitigating it, alleviating the weather's fury.

The wind must have changed directions then, because now it carries the jingle of the tie-rods on the Inn's trees. A crystalline sound that plays out of tune with the deserted parking lot, with the abandoned beach, with the influence of the Po Valley that you continue to feel at your back.

You pass the derelict factory, permitting yourself only a glance at the broken glass, the uprooted bar counter, the empty overturned bottles, and the piles of sand that are trying to reclaim the space that was robbed from them.

You know that at one time people came to visit the sea. When the summer was hot, when they escaped the mugginess of the plain, when surviving was only a problem of the afflicted. Your mother told you. You have seen the images on the school computer, but you have taken them for what they were: snapshots of a myth that was better to forget because beautiful memories only distract you if the present does not match.

Yet you stop. You try to dovetail those images in the abandonment that surrounds you and you simply cannot. You see the fossils of some beach chairs buried in the sand, piles of beach umbrellas of which only metallic skeletons remain, and it seems all is exactly as it should be. What do people have to do with it? What do humans have to do with this cemetery?

"Nothing," you mumble. And maybe that place does not even concern you. You leave behind the little building and arrive at the beach. A dense mist has remained from the rain, an opaque film the color of milk that swallowed the twilight, transforming the landscape into a place out of time.

There is a pier in front of you, a dark path that cleaves the sand and stretches along the beach for close to twenty meters. And at the end of the pier: the Inn. Even if it takes a good minute to understand what you are seeing.

At first glance you thought of a stilt house and a floating barge. Then, little by little, you understand that it is not so: the Inn is composed of a dozen boats united together with scaffolding and gangways, cords and tie-rods, girders and shrouds. Another sliver of the past plunges into your memory: you liked boats, and you and your siblings used to play pirates, especially during the storms. You shake your head. No memories. There is no room for you in the past.

You count at least five sailboats from which the trees sprout with lights, then two large motorboats, maybe some fishing vessels, and the biggest vessel at the center. You are unable to make out the profile of this last one in a precise way—it is surrounded by other boats—but it could be about fifty meters, and to you it seems that its keel is higher by a good meter than the others.

A floodlight oscillates on the roof of what could be the cabin of that ship and it illuminates the entire tangle of boats with its constant motion. You glimpse red stains, then other pallid colors eroded by sea, salt, sand, and time.

The first impression the Inn imparts to you is a friendly disorder and something that perfectly embodies the name of the tavern: those boats have endured, survivors of an ancient era that have found new equilibrium in that bizarre symbiosis. Could it apply to you, as well? You swallow hope as if it were a bitter pill.

You climb the pier that welcomes you with creaks while the yellow of the sun surrenders the passage to the last shadows of the day. Step by step you approach the Inn and you begin to hear voices, even some laughter and clattering from the galley. When a gust of wind whirls around you, soaking you with the foam from low tide, it carries with it the smell of food.

You realize you are hungry. In Bologna, Forlì, and Cesena you ate little and with reluctance. You heard stories about the city that made you very cautious, stories that convinced you to linger there as little as possible. In the Po Valley, you have always settled for some root vegetables and a few provisions bartered from the forest inhabitants, but what you smell now is the fragrance of real food. Cooked food. Meat. Fish. Food that could have the aroma of . . . home?

You chew your lip again in that childish habit you have been trying to stop since you were a little girl. You do not want to—cannot, must not—think of certain things. How do you expect them to be able to accept you after all you have done? Of course, all those with whom you have spoken have told the same story: "They say it's the right place for people who don't know where else to go," or "It's a place where no one cares who you are or what you've done" and so on, but they learned reality the hard way, and it makes no concessions. And above all, the stories are not only stories.

You get to the end of the deck when you realize that it divides into three more narrow walkways, with the end of each one clinging to one of the boats that form the Inn's outer perimeter.

And there you start to see people. They all seem busy on the ships' decks that accommodate them: someone is mopping up condensation, someone is scraping dried salt, others are chatting, drinking, eating. You hear their voices, their sounds, but all around there is an almost unnatural calm. As if the weather, that climate that began to hate human beings, was afraid to push itself that far, up to that strange place where there are people. *People*. Normal people.

You want to escape, leave, return to exile in the Po Valley until you die of hunger or are killed by an illness, the weather, or whatever else. What are you doing there? How did you get involved with these people who manage to take care of banal things like cleaning or chatting, drinking or eating among friends?

Then the floodlight, the one that sweeps the ship in the center of the Inn, illuminates a gold and silver sign that after a few moments switches on and colors the fluorescent letters.

The memories return. The farm. Mom. Dad. Christmas. The lights.

"Inn of the Survivors," you read with a whisper, and those letters, those four words that seem out of place there, twenty meters in the middle of the sea, convince you to enter. After three years, after an exile that took away more than you ever had, after having lost everything, after having thrown *everything* away, you decide to enter.

One step. One step and you leave the pier behind. One step and you climb aboard. You nearly lose your balance: you were not aware that the Inn rocks in that way and it takes a good half minute for your legs to feel certain, your feet to decide to take you forward on the ship's deck.

You keep your head down, the hair that escaped your braid sticks to your cheeks and you flick your eyes first right, then left. You expect that at any moment someone will say something to you, ask who you are, where you are going, what you are doing there. But no one seems to pay you any mind, so you reach the railing of the sailboat's deck. You stop and grab it, taking advantage of the respite to look around.

The boat onto which you have climbed, and no doubt the two closest ones, are the equivalent of small hotels. You peek through the portholes and see berths, hot lights, tiny cabins where shadows move in an intimacy that you have not had for a long time.

"You better hurry." A voice right at your back stops you cold. "They'll be serving dinner soon," it adds. You cannot even move. You stay grasping the railing, tense and ready to spring. Then you hear steps leading away and only after a moment do you manage to glance over your shoulder: nobody. That man said what he needed to and departed. He spoke to you without expecting anything in return, without accusing you, without double meanings, veiled threats, or worse. Not like in the cities where every dialogue becomes a thorny dance that sticks to you like burrs, where speaking with someone you do not know is the surest way to get you in trouble.

"Thank you," you murmur, but you are sure he did not hear you. For a moment, for just a moment, you are almost disappointed.

You raise your head and little by little you decide to learn what is hiding under that sign full of light and hope.

2

THE INN'S ENTRANCE has a red door in the center of a massive wooden wall, covered here and there with sheets of metal. You had not noticed at first, but the ship's deck in the middle of that odd tangle of vessels has been modified, and the inhabitants have ultimately constructed the equivalent of a two-floor apartment up above.

Now that you are here, a gloved hand on the push handle, a foot pointed toward the base of the door, and the rest of your body wanting to flee, you hear the buzz of a little generator army.

They are unlike the gas-powered ones that you had at home, those that sputtered and coughed like asthmatic swine and blew more hot air than your geography teacher. These hiss softly, their breath subdued by the sea that crashes through the Inn's boundaries and slips between the boats.

You have seen some of them in the city and you did not understand how they work, but you know that it is thanks to them that the lights have guided you here and it is also thanks to them that when you open the door, you are overwhelmed by a warm and welcoming atmosphere.

There is a small foyer and what is in essence a short, narrow hallway, a kind of antechamber for what you imagine is the real and true Inn. You close the door behind you and the snarl of the sea, the humidity, the rain, the agitated wind that has whipped you for months on end—all those things remain at the door.

There is a new silence here. Warm. A silence that lets the low clamor of plates and cutlery, and the perfume of *real* food, filter through. You once read that the stomach is a second brain, and in that moment you understand what the person who wrote that meant: you swallow all doubt and indecision, and in their place remains an irresistible attraction towards the world beyond the door in front of you.

When you were little, your father brought you to a slaughterhouse because it was important for you and your siblings to know death as early as possible. To know it in an intimate way. The knowledge that one may derive from confronting it, from seeing it seated at the dinner table together with you day after day, the kind of intimacy that death delivers.

So he brought you all to the slaughterhouse. Because you needed to witness the fate of the animals you had raised, of some of the beasts—your father called them beasts, never "animals"—with whom you played. Because you needed to learn about death. And sometimes, if the day were appropriate, if bad tidings arrived from the forest, the onus was on one of you to kill.

When you entered the slaughterhouse, hundreds of eyes stared back at you. Large, dark pairs of humid globes, all expressionless.

The animals—the beasts—had no real idea what would happen to them shortly thereafter, yet they *knew*. Silent stares. Knowing stares, loaded with a painful awareness that forced you to lower your gaze.

They *knew*, but the pain you saw was not fear. It was comprehension. They seemed to watch you with pity. "We know what you'll do soon. We know what you've had to do every time you've come here. And we're sorry. We're sorry for you."

You look around and you see precisely that. Fifteen people, maybe twenty, who watch you *exactly* as the beasts at the slaughterhouse watched you, with that conscious communion, that pain, all for *you* and nothing to do with *their* fate.

And just like when your father brought you to the slaughterhouse, you welcome this sharing. You welcome those eyes and for the first time in a long while you decide not to lower your gaze; not as a challenge but merely out of acceptance for what is offered to you.

"Over here." For the second time in a few minutes, someone speaks to you. It is the man behind the round counter occupying the center of the room. The dim lights glow brighter there, wrapping him like a warm blanket, while behind him you see a circular table, a dark metal cylindrical drum, and hundreds of bottles and glasses.

You follow the source of that quiet voice, and when you pass the first two wooden tables, you feel that the beasts have quit their stares.

The Inn has a high ceiling a little less than three meters—you have gotten better at gauging heights since you learned to climb trees—from which hang countless different lamps all enlivened with a soft yellow light.

At first glance that space could hold at least a hundred people, but at the moment it hosts significantly fewer.

Step by step, your one boot ringing on the metallic deck, you reach the counter.

The man who called to you awaits with a smile that is neither sad nor happy. He invites you to take a seat on one of the stools and slides over a squat glass full of clear liquid. Then he gestures to it and his smile widens a little.

You want to drink, and all those smells, that multitude of promises and opportunities, are making you courageous. You stretch your lips, trying to remember how to really smile. You free your right hand from your backpack's fasteners. You take the glass and bring it to your mouth.

Surviving is never a sin.

You read it on the coaster that remained stuck to the bottom of the glass. You read it while you drink that sweet liquid, one of the best things that you have ever tasted in recent years. You read it and you drink. In one fell swoop.

Surviving is never a sin.

When you put your glass down, it almost escapes your grasp made clumsy by your glove. Your hand shakes and you feel your eyes widen. A phrase, a simple phrase. Words piled up one over the other, glued to the moist cardboard of the coaster. They nearly make you cry because they seem like the absolution you will never be able to receive.

"That goes for all of us, you know," says the bartender. "It applies to all who come here. Surviving is never a sin. Never. What do you want to eat?" he asks you then, without any change in his tone of voice. As if survival, as if everything that one does to survive, were like asking for a bowl of soup or a steak, some eggs, or whatever else.

"I don't . . ." you start speaking, that growl that you try to clear with a cough. "I can't pay," you start again. "I only have seeds." Then you start to slip off your backpack. Doing something helps you to drive that phrase away from your head. You feel it catch on, take root, but you do not want it to. You cannot let it.

"You don't have to pay with money for your first meal at the Inn," the bartender tells you with his quiet voice and while he does, he reaches a hand over the counter to stop you from taking off your backpack. His touch is gentile, calm. But you recoil. You do not want anyone to touch you because you in turn do not want to touch anyone. Not anymore.

He stays his hand, widens his smile, and withdraws his arm with a serenity that stirs you. In his eyes you read that animal comprehension that forces you to once again lower your gaze.

"Fish soup, stew," he starts to list the dishes, ticking off a finger for each one, "omelet, pork roast or, if you prefer, potatoes, broccoli, zucchini," he uses both hands to rattle off that list.

"Stew." The choice arrives on its own, from the past. It was your mom's favorite dish.

"Stew it is." He turns toward the drum at his back and only in that moment you see it has a monitor. He taps a few digital buttons and with a buzz it comes to life. Maybe a service elevator of some sort. Who knows why, but you had convinced yourself that the Inn is a place out of time and without technology; looking around you, you discover that is not the case. Beyond the shadows, beyond the antiquated furniture, there are traces of a technology in step with the times. Or at least in step with the times of the cities. Outside, in the forest, things are different.

"It'll be a few minutes," says the bartender, turning to you. "More apple juice?" And he points to the empty glass.

"Yes, please," you respond, your voice a little softer. "Where do you get the food?" you ask with both curiosity and suspicion.

"Bartering," he responds while he pours the juice. "We act as an intermediary between the Rimini fishermen and the Po Valley farming community. They're wary, but who isn't? But we have nothing to lose, so they go through us." He tosses that sentence in the middle of the conversation and for some reason you feel it is the most appropriate definition of 'survivors.' People who have nothing to lose. "We talk to everyone. We listen to everyone."

"We?" you ask. You have almost forgotten that you like to chat.

"We," the bartender confirms while carefully moving your glass and wiping down the counter with a rag. "Look," he continues, "there are only a few rules here. People you've met out there, almost all of them, they're passing through. But as long as they're here, they lend a hand. We have places to sleep in these boats, little houses for anyone who wants to stay put." Then he looks you straight in the eye, his hands gripping placemat, silverware, and bread. "We never judge. We never condemn." He stretches toward you and sets the counter. "But we like stories a lot," he concludes with a smile that seems almost mischievous when an electric ding calls him back to the drum. "Ah! Here's your stew!"

It is one of the best things you have ever eaten, yet it is not only the taste. It is good because you are eating it in that place, with other people around you. It is good because you have spoken with someone, because you have asked questions and they have answered, because for the first time in a long time you have heard the word 'we' and because you are daydreaming about what that might mean.

"It's good," you say, and saying it surprises you. But you are happy to have done so.

"Isn't it? Leo's a great cook." He tilts his head back, nodding toward the drum. "There's a kitchen under there," he explains. "Fixing this ship was the first step to build the Inn. Then some fishermen with a boat decided to lay anchor. The rest we bought in Rimini. And so this place was born."

With the last piece of bread, you clean the plate like you did at home, you drink the broth, and you feel your shoulders loosen and the tension slacken. "But what is this place?" The question you asked yourself since you first heard of the Inn of the Survivors, now you ask him.

The bartender looks at you, his elbows leaning on the counter, his hands clasped. "Everyone who comes here has a story to tell. Always. A story that's brought them far from home, a story that made them who they are. A story they're ashamed of or running from, or of who's chasing them." The bartender pauses for a while as if to let those last words sink in. "And more than anything else, this is a place that loves stories," he adds. "So let me ask you: what's yours?"

You open your mouth, then close it. What is he asking you? All of a sudden it is too warm.

You feel the walls close in around you, the barstool jabs into your spine, your backpack heavy. What is he asking you?

Then you realize that you are simply afraid. That the heat, the sensation of suffocating, the stabbing pain in your back, your shoulders torn by the weight of your pack: it all originates from you. No one hates you here, no one wants to harm you.

Surviving is never a sin.

And if it were true? For the first time after three years, you decide to tell your story. And you begin to speak.

3

MY first memory is of when they took my older brother Alan away. He was the oldest. It's clearer than I'd like because it's not a nice memory. It was raining hard. Maybe it was hailing. I spent a lot of my childhood in the rain or hail or snow. Or shut up in the house because it was too dangerous to go out in the wind.

I think I was four years old. We didn't talk about that night. We never talked about it, about my brother or about the men who arrived in a flying vehicle, what day it was or what year it was. After they took him, everyone did their best to forget him and that night.

I was too small to erase people from my memory, but thankfully small enough to be able to tell myself that it was all a bad dream. To believe that it was a bad dream. That my older brother had gone to Parma or some other place in search of fortune.

If you leave a child by themselves with what they've seen, if you don't explain it to them, they'll find a way to come up with something more tolerable. That's what I did. I did it for a long time. I convinced myself that the lights that night were only the beginning of a bad dream, and no one ever bothered to explain to me that that wasn't the case.

They arrived before dinner; I remember that. A flash outside the big living room windows, pouring rain that turned into a kaleidoscope of black and white, vibrations, a rumble that managed to outdo the storm's fury.

They landed in front of the farm, in the large courtyard of gravel and mud that's wedged between the house, stables, and farm shed. They flew in a large, black helicopter and I remember that we all went out on the porch. I was behind mom, curious and a little chilly because the weather had grown strangely colder in the last few weeks. I was behind her while my father and my five siblings were farther ahead.

No one ever came to our hilltop, especially in the evening. Only the Borghi family on Tuesdays—those were the neighbors who dad exchanged vegetables and poultry with—and then the Sassi family on Thursdays for food supplies, generator fuel, and some spare parts. My parents didn't like going to the country in Langhirano and they really didn't like going to the city, so they always tried to have everything they needed.

But that night in the courtyard, it wasn't the Borghi family or the Sassi family. That night three men in green and white uniforms got out of the helicopter and talked with mom and dad. Then they took my brother away without anyone doing anything to stop them. When they went away, when the helicopter left the courtyard, the rain also stopped. The rain stopped, the wind stopped, and the temperature rose a few degrees.

I remember that I walked barefoot in the courtyard, with stones and mud between my toes, and I remember that all of a sudden I wasn't cold anymore. I remember that my mother didn't scold me like she normally would. That night, no one spoke. And I kept looking at the sky, watching the lights of the black helicopter that took my brother away.

Without knowing it, I had witnessed my first CGR, Corrective Genetic Removal. And the thing to *correct* was my brother. Two years later, at school, they explained it to us without mincing words. It was the first time I saw other children other than my siblings, the first lesson where a city official explained CGR to us.

"We don't know when it happened, we don't know why, and we don't know how." I remember that skinny, nervous man. Cesare, I think his name was. He glanced at our teacher. "But we know what the effects are. Your parents will have already explained it to you, but it's good that you understand this. That you understand it well." The thin City councilman paused for dramatic effect.

My parents had never said anything to me. They were simple people and they wanted—hoped for—a simple life. From their point of view, questions and answers were enemies for them to fight every day.

"There's something that binds us to the climate. To the weather. Something that has to do with genetics." The councilman adjusted his round glasses, a ridiculous bone frame with lenses as thick as a finger. "We decide the weather. Our genetic makeup does it. Like we're *made* to do it. There's a relationship that no one has yet managed to understand. A complicated relationship. Some people think that it's because of pollution, others think it was a solar storm." He was saying things I didn't fully understand. But at the same time, it seemed that even he didn't understand. "It doesn't matter. The problem is that our DN… that we've corrupted ourselves. And the climate knows, and it reacts. So, when someone too *flawed* is born, or when someone *becomes* flawed over time, that's when everything gets worse. But not like now." He pointed to the window. It was raining. It was almost always raining. "No. Much, much worse. And the more *flawed* people are all together, the worse things get. That's why the CGR exists. That's why we're here. We make sure that things don't get *too* worse."

The councilman shook hands with the teacher then left in a hurry, seeming to feel uneasy in the midst of so many people. But I would see him again.

That strange revelation didn't make me think of my brother, because in two years I would make up a past I was ok with. One that made me happy. He was safe, had chosen his life, and he wasn't taken away because he was too *flawed*. My brother had nothing to do with things that the councilman had told us.

I found things in history books that my parents had never told me. Maybe they didn't even know, or maybe they expected the school to tell us the truth. Or maybe the truth, on our hill, wasn't so important. You want an example? The Po Valley forest wasn't always a forest. It was a plain once. It was often sunny, hot in the summer and cold in the winter. There was still summer and winter, and even spring and fall. The seasons weren't just a way to divide the year into quarters, they had meaning. They determined the crops, they defined people's lives, how to dress, what to do. All before the climate began to do those *things*. Before the weather took it out on us. The more I learned things about Italy and the world, the more I saw it as an opponent, like something that was an enemy to us.

We played a game at school. The class drew lots to determine which one of us had to wear the rainbow robe. It had velcro patches all over: red, yellow, light and dark blue, green, purple. All the colors. And a black hood that only showed the eyes. The chosen one was the climate, the weather. They wandered the schoolyard and imitated the rain, wind, and hail by making noise, moving their arms, and hitting the doors and windows. Three of us were given the role of "councilmen" and all the others were the *flaws*.

The *flaws* had to hide while the councilmen had to capture them. As soon as they found one, the *flaw* returned to the classroom and the child who played the climate took a patch off. Every patch removed meant that the climate was getting better, that there were fewer and fewer *flaws*. The game ended when the hood was also removed and the climate finally returned to normal. Tranquil, calm, smiling.

Even I played the climate one time. I remember that it was fun to run from one side of the schoolyard to the other, yelling, flapping my arms. I felt free. I could wreak all the havoc I wanted. I could hit doors and windows without anyone scolding me. I was the only one who didn't like to take off the patches: I felt *that* was wrong. Because it felt like I couldn't be who I was, like it was a way not to accept things, not to move on.

When I got back home to our hilltop, a completely different world waited for me. You didn't talk about the climate there, about the *flaws*, the City councilmen, the patches, the Po Valley plain, or the seasons. I didn't talk about them with my parents or my siblings.

I was the youngest of four—five at first—so I asked a bunch of questions on things I learned at school, all the things that they had already supposedly studied. But it seemed that when school finished, they had forgotten everything; seven years of study buried by work in the fields, life at the farm, seeds, animals, the constant fight against a climate that, I discovered time and again, was our enemy.

Maybe they didn't want to talk about it or didn't care about it anymore. What sense did it make to send me to school if what I learned had to stay behind at the foot of the hill? Yet that's what happened. Every day.

But my mother wanted us to learn the names of the trees, plants, and animals: "Did you talk about the forest today?" she asked when I came back from the road, after the bus left me at the start of the hill's rise, after I climbed up the white gravel snake, wrapped up in my pink raincoat.

Sometimes I lied. Even if it wasn't true, I said yes. Because then mom would talk to me about fields, trees, all the beautiful things that she saw on the farm, on the hill, and also in the Po Valley. Sometimes she told me that she wanted another daughter and when I asked her why, she answered with a warm smile. For that I lied. Because I wanted to see mom smile, because I wanted to hear her talk about *beautiful* things.

"Alan wasn't *flawed*, right?" I asked my brother Paolo one time. The councilman had returned to school to tell us what would happen when too many *flaws* were in one place. Short videos, one after another in a sequence that had terrorized my class: twenty-seven-year-olds, many of them coming from the farms. They made us watch how the heat could become so severe it could dry an entire lake over the span of a few weeks, or the temperatures could lower so quickly they could freeze the plants over the course of one night.

"Almost everyone is born *flawed*," the councilman had told us. "But not everyone turns into one. Some changes, biological adjustments, chemical reactions that we aren't able to comprehend. Then the *flaw* manifests. That's why the CGR exists."

That's why the CGR *exists*. All his speeches ended that way, with a celebration of the CGR. He looked like a child trying to justify his latest mischief and so he uses the most absurd examples. Like that one time I tried defending myself by saying that it was the cat who wanted to drink all of the apple juice.

I had returned home with a question in mind that I asked Paolo: "Alan wasn't *flawed*, right?"

At the time, I was convinced that Alan was safe somewhere in Italy. But inside me, from some place under the ashes of the past, smoldered the doubt that his disappearance had to do with the Corrective Genetic Removal. The CGR that the councilman portrayed and defended with a lot of determination.

Paolo had stopped repairing the greenhouse, his even breath visible in the late afternoon cold: "We don't do flaws here. Ever." He kept watching me for a good minute, then resumed working.

Those were strange years for me because I lived in two separate worlds, two worlds isolated from one another that didn't want to—or couldn't—ever meet. On the one hand, the world of the day, of my classmates, the climate game, the history lessons the councilman always taught, and the other of the farm, my world of the night. With dad who worked hard all day. Who spoke little but who tried to show us affection in his gruff way. Who spent more time chatting with the soil than with people. With mom who wanted at all costs for us to understand how important the Po Valley forest was and who seemed to love it as if it were one of her children.

School carried on. I think it was the third year, or maybe the start of the fourth, when the councilman told us for the first time about the *pure*. A short, simple word to describe something so rare.

I didn't immediately understand the contrast to *flawed*, I was too young to do so, but I understood right away that the word *pure* was four letters, just like life. And you could talk about living at home.

Who were the *pure*? Elusive people born with the perfect genetic makeup, with DNA—they had explained to us what DNA was—that was clean, uncorrupted, not polluted from all the things the councilman had explained to us in the first year. And when a *pure* person was born, the climate was aware of it; it clung to their purity, and the atmospheric conditions, the rain, the scorching heat, the chill you couldn't block, all those things vanished and the climate returned to normal.

But the *pure* were rare. Very rare. The religion teacher told us they were holy, and that was why they had chosen a name that had the same number of letters. I listened but didn't understand. For me, *pure* meant *life*. They told us of faraway countries where everyone, or almost everyone, was *pure*. Countries where you didn't have to protect the crops, where animals didn't need protection against the cold, and where it didn't rain for weeks.

We listened. We listened to everything. We listened to those myths, those legends, and some of my classmates talked about it at home and returned to school the next day full of other questions or convinced that the *pure* were a fairytale.

But if it were a fable, an invented story, why had the councilman talked about it? He only told the truth. His entire existence seemed bound in a never-ending search for the truth, so what was the point? Why muddle science with religion? Why did the *pure* appear both in the councilman's lessons and in the religious myths?

That confused me, but I was nine or ten years old, and the confusion wasn't very interesting. In my world, the one of day or night, there wasn't room for uninteresting things.

I've never found a village of the *pure*, a place where one could truly *live*, where they created climate bubbles. At least not in the Po Valley forest. But I understood that they existed, that they had to exist, or that everyone at least believed they did. I understood that when I escaped from home, when I came closer to the forest.

Villages where more children were brought into the world than it was possible to support. They multiplied in those places hoping that sooner or later a *pure* one would be born, a little ignorant creature looking like all the others, a human being that holds within them the possibility of redemption.

Did they live in the past? They were too stubborn to accept that life, now, was of the forest? Were they too desperate to understand that the seasons, the climate like it was written in the history books, would never come back?

Life had a different quality in the villages wedged between the less primitive areas of the forest. The City councilmen didn't go there, and the new tradition, new cults, replaced the Corrective Genetic Removal. Like the shamans, mystics, and mages of the fables they read in school, these people detected the arrival of a *flaw* before it appeared. And, I discovered first-hand, the *flaw* never appeared early. Thirteen, fourteen, fifteen years old. Or maybe later.

So, whoever put the climate at risk, who-ever inadvertently compromised the already fragile equilibrium of that area of forest, was sent away. But to where?

The village elders didn't talk about it and I convinced myself that all of the community members I encountered during my long escape had their rules, their principles.

I know that some shamans order the exile of some *flaws* to the large cities. A sort of pre-cautionary banishment, a way to protect the community.

The cities.

At school they seldom talked about them, and I never understood why. Not even after having seen them with my own eyes.

Have you ever been there?

Cities are the most adaptable manifestation of human nature. Judging from what I studied at school they always have been, but in a dif-ferent way.

Large cities gather hundreds of thousands of people. All together. The councilman explained to us once that the link between the *flaws* and the climate becomes more unstable beyond the point of critical mass. The presence of so many people crowded in such a small space heightens the atmosphere's wrath but at the same time makes it impossible to understand when—and if—a *pure* one is born. Has anyone in the cities renounced hope? Turned a new leaf? Are they happy with what they have? With a hostile but not lethal climate, unexpected but not instantaneous changes, a slow procession—or regression—toward the next evolution? Everyone is welcome in the cities. Everyone is welcome and included in that frenetic organic engine that nourishes them.

They seem like places without a soul that survive because they must, stubborn and adaptable, imparting the unsettling sensation of being able to resist everything.

Did the councilman come from a city? I've seen technologies in Bologna I never imagined. I've seen fragments of the past that history books taught me, but I've also seen the price to pay to allow that stubborn and adaptable world to exist. The city devours you. It absorbs you, consumes you. It feeds on you and after a while you can no longer live without it. That's why I escaped, again.

It took me three years and only after my escape, only after knowing the city lifestyle did I finally accept the truth. Alan, my older brother, wasn't safe. Even if I wanted to believe the tailored reality I invented for myself, Alan couldn't be safe. In the cities, no one was. And Alan had grown up on a farm, in one of the new microcosms that the present offers, one of the satellite communities constructed around City councilmen. Were those a lie, too? A way to survive? A kind of stubbornness?

I often think of Alan. At the farm I was always the little sister and my brothers protected me in their own way. I think of him, the oldest of us, who really felt that he was responsible, that he had to do *something*. I think of when he left, when they took him away. I think about it and I wonder if while they were loading him into that black helicopter he thought about us, about what we would do without him, about all the things he could never do again.

And this brings me back to why I'm here now.

When my mother was pregnant again, I was about to turn thirteen. New possibilities opened up for me: I wouldn't be the youngest for a change, and I would certainly be able to do for my new little brother—everyone at home was convinced that it would be yet another boy— what the others had never done for me. I would teach him, challenge him. About school, about the councilman's words that were sometimes too difficult, about the questions that made sense to ask, and about those things that were better to keep inside. About everything.

It was the last year of school, and my first little brother was about to be born. I had never felt more excited than this.

What did I ask myself afterward? If my parents weren't also looking for a *pure* one, if they weren't also trying at all costs to guarantee the best future for us, rolling the dice on genetics and on fate. But they lost. They lost because no one could imagine what would have happened. Nobody. Not even the councilman knew it. In some way, in the tragedy that I would face, I was the first. Like I was the first to love the climate's role in our school game.

The pregnancy, for my mother, was wonderful. I saw it, without a shadow of a doubt. But dad was worried. Mom wasn't young anymore and having a child with a farm to run could prove to be harder than she could bear.

But that wasn't the case. Mom was glowing and it seemed that the little one that was growing in her womb gave her strength. Instead of exhausting her, instead of taking her breath and will away, the exact opposite happened: sheer energy coursed under her skin.

For me, on the other hand, it was a really bad year. I got sick. I should've finished school and finally begun my life on the farm, but I was so sick that I spent every other day in bed. And when I got up, I felt weak, I had pain everywhere, blurred vision, and little appetite.

The weeks dragged on one by one. Mom's belly grew, the work at the farm went unchanged, and I was bedridden. The doctors also came more than once. Doctors and climatologists. They visited me and checked the weather.

During those long months I understood the sense of what the councilman had tried to explain to us during all his lessons. I understood the symbiosis between human beings and climatic conditions: mom and dad were more worried about the climate experts' verdict than the doctors' diagnoses.

To hear them say "Your daughter has nothing clinically wrong" nevertheless left them with bated breath, stuck. But "We don't detect meteorological anomalies of note" was the magic phrase that could dissolve all their worries. Because what followed was their "You'll see that it will pass, you just have to be patient. It'll pass," they told me. While a change in the climate was too sudden, and for that patience wasn't enough. I knew it and they knew it.

During those long months of bed rest, my brothers showed more affection than they ever had before. A constant pilgrimage brought them to my room. They told me what was happening, the difficulties of working in the fields, how the forest had changed while I "wasted time sleeping," and the Borghi family's new tractor and the new modified seeds that could "even grow in places as humid as a cow's ass." Their profanity made me laugh even if laughing could be painful: something weighed my chest down and I was almost always constricted to rapid and irregular breaths "like a cat with bronchitis."

After five months from the start of the illness, the headaches arrived, and with the headaches, the nightmares.

The days had changed but stayed the same. Time flowed like molasses in a narrow pipe, and I felt the thoughts crowding the tap, pressing up against one another, cramming until it finally made my head burst. And then they dripped out, slowly and painfully.

I don't remember much of the nightmares, but I know that I felt them close by when I was awake. If I think about that time again, before the illness vanished with my escape from home, I can't bring it into focus. A very long, painful day, like a waking fever dream where too many *things* swarmed my brain.

I remember that I wasn't able to separate a single thought. There was Alan, mom, dad, me, the little brother on the way. And then the school, the *flawed*, the *pure*, the climate, the velcro patches, the games, the councilman, the snow, the cities I imagined as enormous creatures without form, the forest, the plant names, the noise of the snow shovel, the hoes, the grumble of the generators, the hot soups, the damp bandages on my forehead when the fever rose, mom's cool hand, dad's calluses that caressed my face, his worried eyes.

And when an idea took over, when an island of thought emerged from that stormy sea that was my mind, it became obsessive. It grew excessively, it swelled and squeezed my skull, pushing to get out even at the cost of splitting my head.

Often, that idea was my little brother on the way. I was convinced it would resolve everything and his presence mixed with all the rest of the hallucinations of a body brought to the extreme.

Thinking about it again now, I should've died. It would've been better for everyone.

Mia was born in September and she wasn't male. Contrary to our beliefs, a girl was born.

I was still in bed, increasingly weaker. And this also contributed to making the event less special than it would have been otherwise. There was nevertheless an electric atmosphere at home, and I remember that in my delirium I managed to find some space for joy: Mia was my little sister. And I, as a result, Mia's older sister. A logic so straightforward to appear almost mystic in the confusion I had in my head.

How many things we'd be able to do together!

But the euphoria was short-lived, at least for me. A week after Mia's birth, I was not recovering, or rather it seemed I was getting increasingly worse. Muscle aches added to the nightmares and headaches. As if a great hand were squeezing me, like a giant wanted to extract every drop of life from me.

It was then that, in that dimension made of suffering and delusions, a part of me realized what had happened: Mia was *pure*.

There was one thing I remember sharply. One thing that no nightmare, no pain, no obsession was able to confuse, or erase, or obscure in the mental confusion of those days. The Sun. That ray of sunshine gleaming through my room's window, a golden beam of light that had infiltrated the curtains to reach my cream-colored sheets.

The heat on my hand, my arm, then my face. That soft caress, that generous communion with pure energy. That splinter of azure, sparkling, brilliant, pure. That fresco beyond the windowpanes that only God could have painted.

I had never seen the Sun. Never. I studied it, of course, I knew that the Sun was certainly there up high above the clouds. I had seen it in photographs, in the councilman's films, and even in some home movies.

But I had never felt its touch in my life. That late-September afternoon, while my mind wandered in the sweaty wasteland of my fugue, I felt it for the first time.

And I swear, I'll never forget it.

That's why even before my brothers rushed into the room to tell me, I realized that Mia was *pure*. Who else could the Sun beckon on our hill? Mia. Only Mia. My little sister arrived serenely.

I thought that in the end it worked out. Alan had been taken away; Mia had arrived. And us in the middle. A simple family that had suffered and now celebrated with an unexpected gift.

I had never been so far from the truth.

So that night, that same night, I wanted to see my sister. I was sick. I could barely stand, but I *had* to see her. I *had* to thank her. She gave me the Sun, she offered me the most beautiful thing I had ever seen or felt.

I don't know what time it was, but I know it was dark. The pain, the nightmares, and the obsessions had returned but it didn't matter. Mia had to know how grateful I was, she had to know right away. It was an urgent matter, something that had to be done at that moment.

I left my room, swaying. I grabbed the wall, passed my brothers' rooms where I could hear their deep breathing, the light snoring of those who worked all day in the fields. On bare feet, I felt the wood cooler than I remembered. Maybe I had a fever, maybe the memory of the Sun continued to warm me.

I also passed my parents' room and I arrived at the little room where Mia was, the same little room where Alan had slept, where my brothers had slept, and where I had slept.

The crib was there. In the glow of the dull streetlamps clinging to the walls of the house, in the soft obscurity made less solitary by the moonlight that managed to find space between the clouds. Clouds made thinner by my sister.

There was Mia. There. Small, still, beautiful.

I approached her, limping, my ears ringing, my hands stretched forward toward the crib. It was as if I saw myself from the outside, as if someone were watching my other self that hobbled toward the purest creature in the world.

Mia was light. She weighed little more than the fat stray cat that occasionally let us pet it when the weather got too cold. She was light, soft, innocent in her little white dress.

I remember that I held her close to me. And then, with all the love and gratitude I possessed, I caressed her face. My hands brushed her skin and that contact, God, that touch washed all the pain, the suffering, the *illness* of the last long nine months.

It was exactly like being caressed by the Sun, but all over. Euphoria, a rebirth. A mind freed from pain, obsessions, nightmares.

This is how flowers must feel the first time they bloom, the first time they show the world their beauty: complete, pure, beautiful.

Then there was a flash of lightning. Far, but so strong as to obscure the light of the streetlamps. And then another. And another. I saw the clouds gather even before feeling the wind. I saw the night blacken and I understood what had happened before even realizing that Mia wasn't breathing anymore.

4

YOU realize you have your hands suspended in midair, a little more than fifty centimeters apart. You feel like you still have your sister in your arms, and though you feel her warmth, you know that it is not true.

You are not on the hilltop, not in the forest.

"I don't know if the City councilmen have a name for people like me," you continue. "I've heard stories of mutations, men and women who react to the *pure* or *flawed*, who are drawn to them." You fix your gaze on something beyond the counter, the bartender, the Inn. Beyond the life you are living.

You bring your hands together and lace your fingers to relieve their aching slumber.

"I don't know why it happened, why me, why Alan, why it happened to my family." You lift the edge of your left glove and you uncover a patch of skin.

Silence around you. The same silence that enveloped your sister's room that night three years ago.

"But I know what I did," you say as you slip off the glove, and for the first time after a long time you look at your hand.

It is pale, like something that has never seen the sun, like the seventeen-year-old girl who lives in the forest, who sleeps outside. Who never takes off her gloves.

You turn it, your palm facing up, open as if waiting for a gift. There are marks there. Marks the color of cream, cream like the sheets where the sun had rested, so long ago. Marks on your fingertips and the top of your palm. Marks where your hand—the hand of a murderer—caressed Mia's skin.

"I consumed her," you mumble, confessing to yourself something that you have always known, but never said. "I took her life and the worst thing is that I felt better when I was doing it. I felt complete. I felt *pure*." You hold still, your eyes glued to those marks, the only things that remain of your sister. "The *flawed* change the climate, contaminate it with their imperfect genes." You hear the words slip out of your mouth like liquid wax. And they burn just as well. "The *pure* improve it, bring back how it used to be." You take your eyes off your hand and as far as you are concerned, you could be alone there. "And then there's me, who takes the most beautiful thing to happen to my family, the *purest* thing, and I destroy it. They had a daughter. They would've had sun, warmth, the richest harvest, the ripest fruit. But I didn't let them." You raise your eyes now. You would like to cry, but you have no more tears. You no longer have anything. "I *consumed* my sister. I killed her."

You shift your gaze to the counter, your left hand abandoned as if it were no longer part of you, no longer yours. "Then I escaped. I returned Mia to her crib, dead, and I escaped. How could I face my mother? Or my father or brothers? I escaped and that's all I do. I escape. I hide. Even too cowardly to die. That's my story." You raise your eyes for the first time since you began to speak. "Did you like it?" Your lips have dried, and those last words are what remain.

You meet the bartender's gaze, and you realize that his eyes have changed. You do not see the mute comprehension of an animal in the slaughterhouse. Now you see something different. Something you know. You see your own eyes, the expression you wore when you wove between the caged cows, with dad. Knowing eyes that have witnessed something.

And you sense others, around you, with those eyes. You turn your head and find sad looks, looks of people on the run, looks of creatures the councilman would perhaps not know how to name. They have lost the game of life. Yet, somehow, they continue to play. Creatures like you.

"This is a place that loves stories," repeats the bartender, his voice full of a pain that hurts because it is like looking at your suffering condensed in a gaze, in a voice, in five words.

Surviving is never a sin, you think.

And maybe, just maybe, you think you could rest here for a while.

The right time—the time it takes—to hear the stories of those who, like you, have survived.

A PARTIAL LIST OF SNUGGLY BOOKS